AN UNOFFICIAL **MINECRAFT** BOOK

# DIARY *OF A*
# MINECRAFT
## *WOLF*

First published by Scholastic Australia Pty Limited in 2024.

The publisher does not have any control over and does not assume any responsibility for author or third-party websites or their content.

This book is a work of fiction. Names, characters, places, and incidents are either the product of the author's imagination or are used fictitiously, and any resemblance to actual persons, living or dead, business establishments, events, or locales is entirely coincidental.

ISBN 978-1-339-04124-7

10 9 8 7 6 5 4 3 2 1          24 25 26 27 28

Printed in the U.S.A.          37

This edition first printing, August 2024

Cover design by Hannah Janzen and Ashley Vargas

Internal design by Hannah Janzen

Typeset in KG First Time in Forever, More Sugar, and White NT.

# DIARY OF A MINECRAFT WOLF

## NETHER GHOST

SCHOLASTIC INC.

"Did you hear? **Winston's back.**"

"Someone told me he thinks **baby turtles** are **evil.**"

The other wolf cubs giggled and **trotted off.** I just **rolled my eyes** as I made my way home. I didn't have time for their immature gossip. I had a **MYSTERY** to solve.

Hidden in my hands was the clue to my next mission—a **NETHER STAR,** left for me by my **nemesis,** the leader of the baby turtles. I'd only just found out I had a nemesis, but I guess now that I'm a secret agent, it comes with the territory. I also have a camouflaged tech suit full of gadgets and a junior agent-in-training called **Brian.**

What I didn't have was any idea what the star means. Nether stars were left by **withers,** but I'd never met a wither. Brian told me nether stars are made from the skulls of wither skeletons. **GROSS.**

**But also neat!** And **unhelpful.**

Maybe if I concentrated real hard . . .

"What have you got there, Winston?" Mom asked when I walked into our cave.

"A nether star. I got it when I solved my last mission with the Drowned and beat the baby turtles yet again." Ever wondered why Drowned attack baby turtles? Well, they're still **mad.**

"Because . . ." she probed.

"Because baby turtles are supervillains,"

I explained to my mom for the hundredth time. "And *I* have to *stop them*."

"It's not that I don't **believe** you," Mom said as she served dinner. "It's just that . . ."

"There's no **proof**," I sighed. It was a very annoying fact that the baby turtles had so far gotten away without leaving **a single trace.** They were always scheming and causing mayhem, but hardly anyone believed me—I was still the only wolf in the entire pack who knew **THE TRUTH.**

"That's why I *have to* follow this latest clue, Mom. My nemesis left it **for me.**"

"Your nemesis." Mom smiled, roughing up my head fur. "It's so cute that you use **code names** for your secret agent friends. Next you'll be telling me one of them is **a player!**"

I nearly **CHOKED** on my food when she said that!

"**Eh, ahem** . . . **HA HA!** Yeah, that would be **funny!**" I said quickly as a cover-up. I hadn't told anyone in the pack that my best friend and secret agent partner, Brian, was in fact, a player. Wolves don't like players. Just like Drowned don't like wolves, and husks don't like villagers. **It's complicated.**

The best thing about Brian, other than his **super cool sword,** was that he knew about the baby turtles and their trickery. And while

all the other wolves still needed
to be convinced, at least my mom
was trying to be **supportive.**

"Okay, so the nether star probably
came from a wither," she agreed.
'I don't want to stand in the way
of your work, Winston, but I'm a
little **worried** about you wandering
around the Nether alone."

"Why?"

"Because **wither skeletons** live in
the Nether, and wolves and wither
skeletons have a **DIFFICULT
HISTORY.**"

Huh. Another complicated mob relationship. Why can't everyone **just be friends?**

"I'll be *extremely* careful,"
I promised Mom.

"I know you would." She smiled at me. "But the wither skeletons may not be friendly. Perhaps you should have Edwina check over your armor and see if there are any **improvements** she can make, to help **keep you safe** in the Nether?" she suggested.

## "THAT'S A GREAT IDEA!"

I **jumped** up and started running for the door but stopped suddenly as Mom **grabbed** the scruff of my neck.

"A great idea **for the morning,**" she corrected. "For now, finish your dinner!"

I **sniffed** deeply, my canine nose picking up all the amazing scents coming from the rest of my dinner.

"Okay, that's an **even better idea.**"

Most wolves think all they need are their claws, their bite, and a strong nose for danger. While those things are useful, a secret agent wolf knows that it doesn't hurt to have an **invention engineer** on your side too!

I entered the Den's lab to find a small wolf with safety goggles on and a pencil behind her ear.

She was carefully pouring a beaker of boiling, red liquid onto a bowl of fruit. As I watched,

the fruit started to **hiss and steam . . .** and then **MELTED.**

"Hmm," the engineer muttered. "Trial number sixty-three. **Heat-resistant fruit** still unsuccessful."

## "HEY, EDWINA!"

She turned around and **squinted** through her goggles, grinning when she saw it was me.

"**Winston!** I heard you're a secret agent now."

I smiled. It was nice to be **taken seriously** for once!

"That's right," I said. "I've actually done **two missions** since you let me field test some of your inventions, and I couldn't have gotten by without your tech suit. Camouflaged armor that blends into fur pixels?

Retractable waterproof helmet with unlimited oxygen? Short-range tracking and teleportation capabilities? **Genius!** I think *every* wolf will be wearing your inventions one day."

"Aww, you're **too kind**." Edwina blushed. She noticed what I was wearing around my neck. "Oh, you've still got the Anti-ADORBS collar. I thought that was **defective?**"

"**NO WAY!**" I insisted. "This is your best invention yet, Edwina. When the hearts explode out of it, it activates a **defense against hypnosis!**"

"Fascinating," she murmured as she **scribbled** in her notepad. "And how did you field-test it? Who tried to hypnotize you?"

**I hesitated.** Nobody else in the pack believed this part.

"Baby turtles," I said.

**She blinked.**

"They use their **cuteness** to **hypnotize** mobs into forgetting all about them and letting them get away. So nobody ever remembers the chaos they cause."

I **held my breath.** I liked being friends with Edwina, and I didn't want her to **laugh** at me. She thought about it for a long time.

"That makes sense," she said finally. She turned back to her workbench. "I was working on a **new prototype** to overcome the defect with the first, but if you think the one you're wearing is already properly tuned . . ."

**"It's perfect,"** I said quickly. "Do you mean you will make **more?"** Imagine if wolves *everywhere* could wear Anti-ADORBS collars and **repel baby turtle hypnosis!**

"I'll **prioritize it** ahead of my heat-proof fruit experiments." We both looked at her bowl of melted fruit. "So, what can I help you with today, Winston?"

I showed her the nether star and explained that it was a clue to my next mission. She put on her safety goggles again and looked at the gem more closely.

"This definitely comes from the Nether," she agreed, "which is a **very dangerous place** for a wolf. I'd like to recommend an upgrade to your tech suit—in particular, I'd like to add **heat-proofing** to your armor."

"Are you sure it's safe?" I eyed her melted fruit again.

"On fruit, no," Edwina said. "On armor, yes. I've been experimenting, and I've developed a **special blend of minerals**—some diamond, some netherite, and a secret ingredient— that combine with the armor to protect it from heat sources. It will keep you safe from all the **LAVA** that's flowing around the Nether."

I gave Edwina my tech suit and she started hammering away at it. I wandered over to the work bench where the new prototype Anti-ADORBS collar was waiting.

"Hey, Edwina? If you don't need this and it still works mostly the same as the old version . . . could I borrow it for **a friend?**"

By the next day, Edwina had finished upgrading my tech suit. I put it back on and was amazed at how well it blended in. Nobody could even see that I was wearing full-body camouflage gear, complete with gadgets and tracking equipment, and now with special **heat-resistant** armor! The only thing it looked like I was wearing was the Anti-ADORBS collar, which wasn't invisible like the rest.

I didn't mind, though, even if
the other cubs said it looked like
I was someone's pet. I wasn't
going anywhere without it after
seeing what the baby turtles were
capable of!

*Besides,* I thought with a grin,
*I know I'm not anybody's pet,
because I have* **my own pet**
*that no one else knows about!*

"Hey, Brian!"

My **pet player** and **best friend**
was in the exact spot he'd said
he would be. When we first met,

I tamed him by letting him throw me bones, and now we are secret agents together. He's **quite good** at secret agenting, but I try not to leave him on his own too much. Sometimes he just disappears and, really, he's just **so helpless** without me.

"Hi, Winston. What do you think of my **nether portal?**"

He stood back so I could look. He had **stacked** blocks of **black obsidian** into a big frame. It looked like a **DOORWAY.**

"It would probably be better if

it had a **door**," I said helpfully—
maybe players don't know how
doorways work. "How else are you
meant to **open it?**"

"With *this*." Brian took a flint from
his pocket. "Stand back."

"I don't know, Brian," I said
uncertainly. "I don't think it's **safe**
for us to be **playing around with
fire.**"

"Normally, yes, but I read online
that the way to open a nether
portal is by **igniting** it with fire.
So, here goes . . ."

He lit a small flame and set the inside of the obsidian frame alight. Immediately, a **swirling, purple vortex** filled the doorway. Both Brian and I stared with our mouths open.

"**Whoa** . . ."

# IT WAS SPECTACULAR!

"I'm so glad that turtle left you a nether star," Brian said excitedly. He was **grinning.** "I've never played the

Nether. This mission is going to be **AWESOME!"**

I frowned at him. Brian is a very good player most of the time, but he gets a bit *confused*. He seems to think Minecraft is **a game!**

"You need to **focus,** Brian," I said sternly. "This is serious. Something sinister may be afoot. We need to stay sharp."

"Speaking of the mission, do you still have that nether star?"

"Huh? Oh . . ." I checked all the

hidden pockets of my tech suit. The nether star was **nowhere to be found.** I tried to remember when I had last seen it. "I must have dropped it in Edwina's lab. **WHICH REMINDS ME!**"

I pulled out the spare Anti-ADORBS collar and presented it to Brian.

**"THIS IS FOR YOU!"**

"You want me to wear *a collar?* Winston, we've talked about this—I'm not really your pet. And my name isn't really Brian. It's actually—"

"Okay, Brian, listen," I interrupted, because he can go on and on for days if I don't keep him focused. "This is **very sophisticated** new technology from the best inventor in all of Minecraft. It will keep you from being hypnotized by baby turtles."

"Oh. Well, that could come in handy," Brian said,

accepting the collar and putting it on.

"I don't think any other player would have this item. I always find **rare,**

**cool stuff** when I'm with you.
THANKS, WINSTON!"

I smiled. Now that we were both protected from hypnosis, we were ready to go. I turned to look at the swirling purple of the nether portal again.

"Is it safe?" I asked.

Brian shrugged. "Probably not. **Still want to go?**"

"DEFINITELY."

# WEDNESDAY

## STILL MORNING

**"ARGH!** Definitely not! Definitely NOT!"

Brian and I **tumbled** out of the nether portal into a dimension unlike anything I'd ever experienced.

I didn't like it.

"Why is it so **HOT?**" I demanded. What kind of awful place was this?

Heat! Fire! Reddish darkness! And did I mention **HEAT?**

"Probably something to do with all the **lava,**" Brian said. He wiped some sweat off his brow. "The Nether is full of the stuff."

But I was hardly listening. I was too hot! Under my shaggy fur, I felt like I was **melting.**

"Whoa, Winston, you're breathing pretty hard. Are you okay?"

I shook my head. I was *not* okay **AT ALL.** I now understood why everyone back at the Den said the Nether was no place for a wolf.

"I'm sure I have some water in here . . ." Brian said, staring into space.

"**Yes!** Water, please, yes—**SO THIRSTY!**"

I watched desperately as Brian pulled a **bucket of water** out of thin air and set it down in front of me, and I was eager to lick it up and feel the delicious, cool wetness in my throat. But as soon as the bucket touched the ground, **the water disappeared!**

"**WHAT?! NO!**" I yelled. "Please, **try again!**"

Brian tried again. And again, the water disappeared. I couldn't believe my burning eyes.

"Oh, that's right!" Brian realized, smacking his forehead. "Water **can't exist** in the Nether. It's too hot—it just **evaporates** immediately."

I **stared** at him. "**YOU TELL ME THIS NOW?!**" I demanded.

Overhead, even the dark sky looked like it was **burning.** That horrible sky was going to be the last thing I ever saw. I gasped, inhaling hot, steamy air. I was literally being **cooked alive! ROAST WOLF,** coming right up!

"Sorry, I didn't think it would be relevant."

It was hot, too hot.

"Brian," I **rasped.** "Can't . . . go on. This is the end . . ."

"No, I'm pretty sure this is the Nether. I haven't played **the End** yet."

**Always with the playing.**

"Sorry . . . to leave you . . . all alone," I whispered as I started to close my eyes.

"Winston, I think you're okay. You're just a bit **overheated**."

"I can see the light . . ." I couldn't *really*, but I know that's what you're supposed to say in these situations. I **flopped** into Brian's arms.

"HOLD ME!"

Surprised, Brian caught me, and his hand **bumped** some invisible switch on my tech suit. Then, just as I thought it was all over . . . **the heat was gone.**

Like, I couldn't feel it. At all.
I opened one eye, confused. Had I *already* been respawned?

Nope. The sky over my head was still a dark, rusty red, and Brian was still holding me like a pile of laundry.

**I was alive.** But how?

"What's this **hard lump** just here?"

Brian asked, squinting to try and see the camouflaged switch amongst my fur pixels.

Then I understood.

"**EDWINA!**" I yelled, jumping out of Brian's arms. "You really are a genius!"

"I thought you liked to call me Brian. But I'm okay with '**genius.**'"

"Not you," I laughed. "Edwina made some improvements to my tech suit, including heat-resistant technology. All I had to do was

**activate** the shielding!"

I jumped around on the molten rock
and my feet didn't burn at all. **SO.
AWESOME.**

"You're welcome, I guess," Brian said.
"Does this mean all that **DRAMA**
just now was **for nothing?**"

"Huh? Drama?" I thought back over
my **very reasonable** behavior
and wasn't sure what he was talking
about. "Stop wasting time, Brian.
Let's get on with our mission!"

# WEDNESDAY

"I think it's **this way**."

"No, look, it's **that way**."

"Wait, it's spinning again . . . okay, north is **over here**."

"All right, let's go. Oh no, hang on. North has moved around again."

"North can't just 'move around,'

Winston. Anyway, the compass doesn't point north."

Now that my temperature control was activated, **navigating** the Nether was our next problem. Neither of us had been here before. The landscape was dark, stark, and just plain **unfriendly.** Brian had taken out his compass, but it was no use. The needle **SPUN WILDLY.** In short, we really didn't know where we were going.

We **clambered up** a rocky, reddish hill and Brian put his compass away.

"Remind me, what exactly did the note from your baby turtle friend say?" Brian asked.

"He's my baby turtle nemesis," I **sniffed.** "*Not* friend. And it didn't say much. Just 'see you soon.'"

"And somehow you thought that meant 'Hi, Winston, come to the Nether and **get toasty!**'"

"No, there was also a nether star in the package and that was my clue to come here."

"Would have been handy if you'd

**kept that.** Maybe we were supposed to make **a beacon . . .**" Brian said.

I still couldn't remember exactly what I'd done with it. The last place I remembered having it was in Edwina's lab, but then I'd gotten distracted with the spare Anti-ADORBS collar.

Brian was looking around.

"I can't see any structures from here," he said. "Just red dirt, lava, scorched sky—you know, the usual. Although . . ." He squinted hard at the horizon. ". . . There might be some **movement** over that way."

I squinted with my wolf eyes, which are a bit sharper than player eyes. Yes, there was definitely something moving. **Something fast.**

"Huh," I said with interest. "It looks like a group of **hostile mobs** sprinting this way."

Brian **stared** at me.

"So . . . we're **UNDER ATTACK?**"

"Seems that way."

"So . . . RUN?"

"Yeah, I think that's a good plan,"
I agreed, and we turned and
**BOLTED.**

We were **hopelessly lost,** but
luckily some of our footprints were
still visible in the
red dirt,
so we
followed
those.

**"WHAT ARE
THEY?"** Brian
yelled as we ran.

I glanced over my shoulder at the mobs that were quickly gaining on us.

"Uh, they're black . . . and bony and **scary-looking.**"

**"Wither skeletons? WE'RE BEING ATTACKED BY WITHER SKELETONS?!"**

I'd never met a wither skeleton, but I thought that this was the welcome I should have expected. My mom and Edwina **warned me** that wither skeletons aren't fond of wolves, and most mobs also don't like players. At least, in a minute, this wouldn't be a problem—we'd just jump into our portal and teleport back home to the **safety** of the Overworld.

Any minute now . . .

The hostile mobs were getting closer.

**It shouldn't be far . . .**

I was following our footprints, so I knew we were going in the **right direction,** but I still couldn't see the nether portal. Then the footprints suddenly **ran out.**

And there was still **NO PORTAL.**

"Wait, **where did it go?**" Brian
asked, stopping and looking around.
"Did we get **lost?**"

"We followed our own tracks,"
I said. I backed up and **sniffed** the
ground. Yes,
there was
our scent,
**fresh** from
this morning.
And those
scuff
marks
looked

to be where we landed, but there was no nether portal. Just more scuff marks, which the wind was already **blowing away**. "It is a bit windy . . ."

"Do not suggest *the wind* blew it away, Winston. It's **made of obsidian!**" Brian looked around. "It must have been **DESTROYED.**"

"Or we **misplaced** it," I reasoned. "Just like the nether star."

The cloud of dust from the sprinting wither skeletons was catching up, and there was nowhere to go. By now, my sharp **wolf hearing** was picking up the grinding clunks of their burned, **withered bones.**

**Grimly,** Brian looked at me.

"I guess it doesn't make a difference now," he said as the group of wither skeletons approached.

**"WHO ARE YOU?"** boomed the wither skeleton standing at the head of the group.

**"Who are you?"** I shot back.

"Winston, you can't answer back like that to *a captain,*" Brian **hissed.**

"How do you know he's a captain?" I asked while the wither skeletons glared at me. Every single one had a sword.

Brian pointed to the leader's name badge. I **gulped.**

"Oh. I see your name badge now. **'Captain Hugo.'** Nice to meet you."

"Who are you," Captain Hugo **boomed** again, "and what are you doing here? Wolves and players are **NOT WELCOME."**

Well, that seemed a bit unfair, but Brian nudged me to stay quiet.

"He's
Winston
Wolf, and
I'm—"
Brian
started.

"That's Brian," I added helpfully.
"We are here on a mission."

The wither skeletons pointed
their swords **suspiciously.**
Hugo frowned.

"What mission?" he demanded.
"We have enough trouble with our
**HAUNTED FORTRESS.**"

Haunted fortress? Brian looked at me.

"Maybe this is our mission?" he suggested. I nodded **eagerly.**

"**Yes!** We would like to help you with your haunted fortress."

Captain Hugo didn't look convinced.

"We don't need help from wolves and players," he said.

"What about help from **SECRET AGENTS?**" I asked. "We happen to be **very experienced** secret agents. So far we have helped the wolves and the Drowned."

All the wither skeleton warriors whispered to one another. Captain Hugo thought about it.

"I **doubt** you are **good enough agents** to solve our problem," he said finally. "We have been **bothered for days** now by an entity no one can see. Our fortress is **HAUNTED** by a spooky presence that makes scary noises, steals materials when no one is looking, and is even blocking off passageways."

"Some of us—not me—are **a little bit scared,**" another wither skeleton admitted.

I nodded. I could certainly understand being afraid of a **troublesome nether ghost!** But on the inside, I was getting **excited.** Missing items, invisible foes, a fortress with blocked passageways, and creepy noises coming from nowhere? This was *definitely* my kind of mystery!

Plus, the baby turtle leader had given me a nether star **for a reason.** Maybe this mission had something to do with it?

"We will help," I promised Captain Hugo.

The wither skeletons seemed much less excited about this than I was.

"None of us are happy about you being here," Captain Hugo warned me. "Either you **solve this mystery** quickly . . . or you are **out of here.**"

He started leading us in the opposite direction to where we were originally headed. Soon, the dark sky cleared enough on the horizon for us to see **a lava lake,** followed by a big, imposing structure on the other side.

# A NETHER FORTRESS.

Inside, the nether fortress was just as **cool-looking** as the outside, with lots of twisty passageways and rough-hewn walls made of warm, reddish-black stone. Aside from the whole **volcanic vibe,** it kind of reminded me of the **Den.**

But this didn't feel like my pack's nice, safe, underground home. It was clear all the wither skeletons were **on edge.** Once Captain Hugo and his warriors led us inside, the other wither skeletons stared. Some frowned or bared their sharp teeth. One even **gnashed** at us and hissed, "Take your **pet wolf** and **GET OUT OF HERE, PLAYER!**"

*"Actually,"* I said, **very politely,** "this player is *my* pet. I **tamed** him."

The mean wither skeleton didn't seem to care.

"Maybe just leave them alone, hmm?" Brian said, pulling me away.

"Yes, many of our citizens do not welcome players to our home," Captain Hugo explained. "Players often come to the Nether to **cause trouble**—stealing minerals, hurting local mobs, and destroying our buildings. We *do not* like it."

Captain Hugo led us around so we could get a good view of the fortress. There were lots of passages, and everything seemed to take a long time to get to, with lots of bends and dead ends.

"You wither skeletons really like going **the long way,** huh?"

"No, this is what I was telling you about," Captain Hugo explained. "These passageways all used to be **straight and direct.** Now someone has started **blocking off** certain parts of the fortress, creating all these **dead ends.**"

"We **HATE** being inconvenienced," another wither skeleton added grumpily.

"Are you sure no one has seen the culprit?" I asked. "This is **major reconstruction.** Someone must have seen or heard them moving all the blocks."

Captain Hugo gave me a **withering** look. **HA—WITHERING!**

"If someone had seen the culprit, we wouldn't think the fortress was haunted," he said.

"Besides," one of his warriors added, "wither skeletons know how to **take care of troublemakers.** If anyone had seen anything . . ."

They all showed me **their swords. I GOT THE MESSAGE.** I was about to reply that maybe they hadn't seen anything because it didn't look like wither skeletons

had **actual eyes,** when I heard
a sound.

# WWWHAAAAA-
# CHOOOOOOOHHHHH!

"**That's it!**" Captain Hugo's warriors
all whispered. "**IT'S BACK!**"

# HIIISSSSSSSSSSSSS!

# BANG! BANG! BANG!

## WWWHAAAAA-CHOOOOOOHHHHH!

The bizarre, **ghostly sound** echoed through the blocked and twisty passageways, making it impossible to tell which direction it had come from. It was **definitely spooky!**

I'd thought wither skeletons were pretty scary, with their bones on display and their sharp weapons, but when they heard that awful noise, all the civilian wither skeletons around me **SCURRIED** home. The warriors shivered nervously, their black bones rattling. Captain Hugo looked **disgusted.**

**I gulped.** Anything scary enough to scare wither skeletons was worth being at least *a tiny bit* afraid of, right?

**"It's all right, Brian,"** I declared loudly. "You don't need to be scared."

Brian frowned at me. **What?** I was just being **supportive.**

"What can you tell us about the layout of the fortress, Captain Hugo?" he asked. "What passageways have been blocked?"

"Most of the blocked passageways lead to **the lower levels.** It's very warm down there, because of the **LAVA FLOWS.**" The captain shrugged. "I don't know why a ghost would want to hide near lava though."

Hmm, not a very helpful clue. Whatever this mob, or being, was, it made strange loud noises, liked warm lava, and reconstructed fortresses without being noticed.

Very mysterious!

Maybe once I knew what it **wanted,** I'd be able to work out **who they were!**

"You said they were also **stealing** things," I mentioned. "That stuff has been going missing. **What stuff?"**

"All sorts. Lab equipment, some crafting materials. and even rare mineral blocks from our secret stores."

"Yes, in fact, Professor Crush reported more of his **beakers**

**and lab gear** missing just this morning," another wither skeleton warrior told me. "And every day there are  less **netherite and diamonds** in our storage caverns. Oh! And we're also missing a **smithing table**."

How strange. I wouldn't have thought ghosts **cared** about diamonds and glass beakers!

Despite *hours* of following Captain Hugo around, we never seemed able to find an unblocked passage. Brian had offered to break down some walls for them, but the captain had gotten **angry** and said that all players ever wanted to do was **wreck things.**

Now it was the next morning. I'd slept on the floor, which

suited me fine, but players are **very sensitive** and prefer beds. However, Brian had explained to me that beds **EXPLODE** in the Nether—**fancy that!**—and he'd **vanished** for the night. He did that sometimes. Just completely disappeared. Don't ask. Players are **weird.**

Anyway, the floor was warm and comfy. I **stretched** and looked around. Captain Hugo wasn't around, and it seemed very early in the morning, so I thought I might do some **exploring** while the wither skeletons slept. Who knows, maybe I'd find **more clues** without all the crowds going about their daily business.

So I got up and set off. The passageways were dim and just as twisty as the day before. It would be very easy to get lost. Lucky I had my great **wolf eyesight** and **sense of direction.**

As I walked, I started wondering about the objects the ghost had been taking. A smithing table.

Rare and valuable blocks with strong properties. Lab equipment. It was hard to say whether the troublesome ghost was interested in **performing experiments,** or trying to **build armor.**

Maybe both?

But how could it be **both?**

# "WOLLLFFFFFF . . ."

I frowned and looked around at the closed-in walls. Was that a **voice?** A ghostly, spooky voice? Surely not . . . it was just the breeze.

Hang on. A breeze in an **underground fortress?**

# "AAAAGGGGEEENTT WOLLLFFFFFF CUBBBBB . . ."

I shuddered. That wind definitely sounded like a voice, **talking to me.** And it was coming from the dark passageway to my right.

Wait . . . that passageway hadn't been there a minute ago, **had it?**

No wonder the wither skeletons were fed up with this entity.

It was making it very hard to get around the fortress without becoming **HOPELESSLY LOST!**

**"WOLLLFFF . . .**

**FOLLOWWWW . . ."**

"Follow? Well, all right then," I said, and turned to go down the dark passage to my right. Maybe the ghostly voice wanted to **help me** solve the mystery!

"Winston? **What are you doing?"**

I stopped and looked behind me.

Brian was back.

"I . . ." But the voice was silent now.
"I thought I heard something.
A spooky voice telling me to follow."

We both listened, but the voice didn't
come back. Brian **shook** his head.

"Following a disembodied voice into a
dark passage in a haunted fortress,
**alone?"** Brian
shooed me
away. "How
would you even
**survive** without
me, seriously?"

I shook my head. It was cute how Brian thought *he* was the one **looking after me,** when I was clearly the **more capable one.**

"I've been thinking about the different **types of items** missing," I said. "Some stuff is for crafting armor, while other stuff is for running science experiments."

"I agree," Brian said. "And that's not the only thing that's **shady.** I went back to the spot where our portal disappeared, and we **didn't lose it**—it was **DISMANTLED.** I found some of the obsidian blocks, **scattered and buried!**"

"**Buried!** So someone is trying to stop us from returning home."

"Well, they're trying to stop *you*," Brian reasoned. "I can leave whenever. I just have to **switch off my PC.**"

"**Your peace-what?**"

"Never mind." Brian shook his head. "My point is, you need to be **more careful.** No more wandering off down dark, creepy passageways on your own."

I followed my friend back up to the upper levels. **He was right.** I didn't know why my nemesis had left the nether star to summon me here. All I really knew was what the note had said:

To: Agent wolf cub
From: Your nemesis

**SEE YOU SOON . . .**

## "ARGHHH! THOSE ROTTEN GHOSTS!"

Brian and I looked at each other. Someone was mad—**very mad.** We hurried through the twisting passageways until we arrived at the source of the yelling. Captain Hugo, backed by his wither skeleton warriors, was trying to calm down a **mad-looking** wither skeleton wearing a **welding mask.**

"Arnie, they *can't* have taken **all of them."**

"EVERY SINGLE ONE!" Arnie fumed. "Do you know how *long* it takes to craft **that many helmets?** How many shells I had to collect to make them? Now I'll have to start **ALL OVER AGAIN!"**

Based on the room we were in, I figured that Arnie was the nether fortress's **armorer.** Hanging on the walls were shields and weapons of various kinds. But one whole set of shelves was **empty.**

"They took your helmets?" I asked. Everyone turned to stare at me.

"All but the one I'm wearing," Arnie said. He showed me what it looked like. "No one saw a thing."

"Did you leave the room?"

Arnie looked **confused.**

"No . . . so I *should have* seen them.
**I don't understand!**"

Very suspicious indeed! His memory
seemed **faulty.** How could he forget
what had only *just* happened?

"You said you were a secret agent
and you were going to help us with
this haunting problem," Captain
Hugo said angrily to me, drawing his
sword. "Instead, *more* stuff has
gone missing!"

All the wither skeletons whipped out their swords and pointed them at me as well.

## SO TOUCHY!

"We've only been here for **one day**," I reminded him. "I'm still trying to solve the mystery."

Captain Hugo turned his sword to the door to show me the way out. I **sighed** and **slunk** to the exit, Brian behind me. Now I'd **never** be able to find out why the baby turtle leader had **summoned me here**.

# WAIT A MINUTE . . .

"What did you say the helmets were **made of?**" I asked.

Arnie shrugged.

"There are a few kinds, but these ones were all made of **turtle shell.**"

I looked expectantly at Brian. He **shook his finger** at me.

"Oh no, I know what you're thinking," he said. "And it **can't be,** for three reasons. One, baby turtles have no reason to steal their own shells. Two, we know that baby turtles **HATE** lava, so this is the last place they would want to come. And three, it can't be baby turtles, because it was baby turtles **last mission, AND THE ONE BEFORE THAT!**"

"Anyway," Captain Hugo said, "the culprits obviously are some kind of **ghostly mob,** because no one ever sees them and we keep hearing odd, spooky noises in the fortress."

"**Hmm.**" He was right that no one had seen the troublemakers and the noises were very ghostly, but that didn't mean for certain that the fortress was haunted. "Tell me again what was stolen?"

"Stuff for crafting, and stuff for experiments," Brian said **impatiently.** "And now turtle shell helmets."

Stuff for crafting . . . and stuff for experiments . . . on turtle shell helmets . . . in the lava . . . with all the passageways blocked off for privacy . . . and nobody seeing a thing . . .

**OH.** Suddenly, I knew **exactly** what we were dealing with.

Brian was watching my face.

"You just worked it out, didn't you?"

"I did," I confirmed **proudly.**

Captain Hugo, Arnie, and the wither skeleton warriors crowded closer in anticipation. I took a deep breath.

"I have **SOLVED THE MYSTERY!** I can now reveal that the culprits behind your haunted fortress are, in fact . . ."

## "BABY TURTLES!"

I looked around **proudly.** The others blinked in confusion.

## "WAIT, AGAIN?"
Brian said.

"What's he talking about?" asked Arnie.

"Did he just say our nether fortress is haunted by **INFANT REPTILES?!**" exploded Captain Hugo.

I sighed. No one *ever* believed me. I would have to explain. Luckily, I kind of **liked explaining.**

"Your fortress **isn't haunted**," I said, "but it is **INFESTED**, with the greatest villains in all of Minecraft—**baby turtles.** I should have guessed as soon as we arrived, from **all the lava.**"

"But, Winston, we know from our last mission that baby turtles are afraid of lava," Brian reminded me. "When I threatened them with it, they swam away. They **can't survive** a bath in molten goo."

"**EXACTLY!**" I waved my paws excitedly at the empty shelves. "That's why they're here, and that's why they stole all the turtle shell helmets. They're **experimenting**."

"Experimenting? Like, science experiments?" Captain Hugo asked.

"Kind of. After their run-in with Brian and me at the Drowned city, their leader knows that we discovered lava to be their **weakness.** So I bet they've come here to see if they can make themselves **heat-resistant."**

"That's why they've taken lab gear like beakers and tongs—to handle the lava safely," Brian realized. He looked at the empty shelves. "And they would use the turtle shell helmets to run trials so they don't **burn** their own shells."

**"Rotten turtle ghosts,** wasting all my good helmets," Arnie muttered. "Well, how would they make themselves lava-resistant?"

I thought of Edwina trying to make heat-resistant fruit as well as armor. I remembered her **special blend** for my armor upgrade.

"The netherite and diamond blocks," I explained. "That's why the turtles took those materials. They're using the smithing table they stole and experimenting on the shell helmets. With the right combination, they could make themselves totally heat-resistant. All they need is the **final secret ingredient.**"

Then they would never need to fear lava again.

"If they're already experimenting, it's only a **matter of time** before they discover what the secret ingredient is. Do you think that's why they chose the lower levels, Winston?" Brian asked. "Because of the lava flows, and for privacy?"

*Absolutely.* And I also thought that it was why they kept blocking off passageways—to try and keep the wither skeletons who lived in the fortress from discovering what they were up to. I was about to answer, but Captain Hugo interrupted.

"I don't think any of this is accurate,"

he said. "We haven't seen **a single turtle.** Have we?"

All the other wither skeletons shook their heads. "Well, the thing is . . . unless you're wearing one of these, you might not remember," Brian said, showing them the collar around his neck. "Baby turtles have a sort of **HYPNOSIS** they can perform on anyone who sees them. Something about how **cute** they are." He shrugged. "I know, it's not in any of the guides I read online. But it's true."

"You mean, the baby turtle ghosts

might have stolen all my helmets, **right under my nose?**" Arnie asked. "And I would have seen it and . . . **done nothing?** And then **FORGOTTEN?**"

"Not ghosts, but yes," I said. "Baby turtles are extremely tricky. If they are running experiments in your fortress's lower levels and are stealing from your workshops and storage rooms, many wither skeletons might have seen them and been hypnotized into forgetting. You need to be **extra careful.**"

Captain Hugo still wasn't convinced.

"All this *may* be true, and we *may* be being **terrorized** by reptile babies, but you still haven't explained the noise. How are they making the **ghostly noises** we keep hearing?"

I hesitated. That was one thing I couldn't figure out. The echoey wailing, banging, and hissing of the fortress's supposed ghost was not a normal set of sounds made by baby turtles. They weren't really normal for *any* mob I'd encountered.

WWWHAAAAA-CHOOOOOOHHHHH!

# HIIISSSSSSSSSSSS!

# BANG! BANG! BANG!

My wolf ears **pricked up.** There it was again! **PERFECT TIMING!**

"Here's our chance to find out!" I said, bounding out of the armory. "Let's catch them in the act!"

**"Winston, wait!"** Brian hurried to keep up.

"No, I like this idea!" yelled Captain Hugo. "Wither warriors, **let's find those ghosts!"**

I didn't bother reminding him that he should be looking for living baby turtles, not ghost ones, and just enjoyed the chase. We wolves **LOVE RUNNING,** and the cavernous passageways of the nether fortress felt just like the Den, only warmer. Following the sound, I took a turn and ran down a sloped tunnel. The deeper I went into the reddish earth, the warmer it got.

Weird that I hadn't run into any dead ends yet.

"Winston, **slow down** for me," Brian called from farther back.

I could only just hear him over the **banging noise.** What were the baby turtles up to? I **COULDN'T WAIT** to find out.

"Remember, someone **destroyed** our nether portal. Someone is trying to **keep you here—**" Brian yelled.

"There's **a fork** up ahead!" I called back. I could see better in the dark than he could, and I was farther in front. "It goes in three directions."

"We will go straight ahead!" Captain Hugo said. He and his wither skeleton warriors were **fast** and overtook me to run down the middle tunnel.

"**Okay!** Brian, you **go right**," I shouted. "**I'll go left!**"

"**WAIT!**" Brian called again.

But I veered off, put on **a burst of speed,** and heard his footsteps get quieter. He must have done as I'd told him.

My narrow tunnel went down **steeply** and curved into a

sharp turn, then another, and then it forked and I leaned left again. Then it got narrower, and then came another turn, and then—

"**DEAD END!**" I pulled up short before my nose could be **flattened** by the stone wall. I hadn't seen any dead ends for a while and had forgotten they were a problem in this fortress.

Oh, well. I could just backtrack and meet up with Brian. I turned around.

**And froze.** A baby turtle stood in the passageway.

It grinned at me. **SO PETRIFYINGLY CUTE.**

And before I could say or do anything, it **whipped** a giant stone block out of nowhere, and threw it on the ground. It **filled** the entire passageway . . .

**. . . TRAPPING ME IN THE DARK.**

"HELP! Help, I'm trapped!"
I **howled** at the top of my lungs.

I knew my distress call could be
**heard for miles** by any other
nearby wolves, carried by the
wind to their well-trained ears.
But, unfortunately, there was **no
wind** in the lower level passages
of the nether fortress. Even more
unfortunately, there were no other

wolves in the Nether. And Brian and the wither skeletons would be too caught up in the chase to come looking for me. I was **alone,** and I was trapped in an underground room. I started to **PANIC**. The only way back was blocked with rock, and no matter how hard I scratched at it with my claws, it wouldn't budge.

Those **rotten baby turtles!** I realized that this must have been their plan **all along**. That's why their leader left me that note and the nether star—to **LURE ME HERE**. That's why our portal home wasn't there when we went back for it—they had dismantled it. The baby turtle leader knew I would follow the clues and come here, and it knew I would follow the noises down here on my own, trying to be a hero. I'd run right into its **TRAP.**

"HELP! HELP!! HELP!!!!!!"

I **whined,** scratching uselessly. Then I stopped to listen. **Nothing.**

I tried to take some big breaths. I *had* to get out, or the baby turtles would continue with their villainy and complete their plan.

I sniffed the walls. **No gaps.** I sniffed the floor. **Solid.** I sniffed my, uh, upper leg. You know, for good luck. But as I did, my nose bumped a button I'd never noticed before, and a strange, pale blue light bulb activated.

Weird. At least it gave me a bit of light to work with. It also emitted an

**odd sound** that annoyed my ears, but I was able to ignore it easily enough. Not sure why Edwina would include that feature on an otherwise perfectly functional tech suit.

I went back to sniffing the walls, trying to find a way out.

## CHINK . . . CHINK . . .

I paused when I heard yet another odd noise. This sounded like **metal tools** hitting rock. I looked around, but there was no one in the tunnel.

At least, not on *this side* of the rock.

"HEY!" I yelled against the wall. "I'm in here!"

"Winston?" I heard Brian call from the other side. "STAND BACK!"

I did as he said, and he CRASHED THROUGH the rock with his axe. Behind him, the wither skeletons were watching, unsure whether to be angry about his destruction or impressed. Maybe both.

"BRIAN!" I said joyfully. "I thought I'd be **trapped forever.** How did you find me?"

"Your **beacon**," Brian replied, putting his axe down. He pointed to the glowing, pale blue light on my upper leg. "We started to hear an unusual beeping emitting at a regular frequency, so we regrouped and followed it. Didn't *you* activate it?"

I looked at the light **blankly.**

"Beacons are made from **NETHER STARS.** I suppose you didn't **misplace** yours after all. I could see it glowing through the rock as I got closer. Although, they normally have to be on pyramids to work," Brian continued.

I **gasped.** EDWINA! So I *had* left it in the lab.

"She must have built it into my tech suit," I realized. "If anyone can get around the rules, it's Edwina."

"Make sure you thank her later," Brian said. "In the meantime, don't we have baby turtles to stop?"

I **grinned** with all my wolf teeth.

## "DEFINITELY."

Brian picked up his axe and looked at Captain Hugo. "May I?"

"Oh, fine," he said **grudgingly.**

The wither skeletons raised their swords, **inspired.** I flexed my claws. Brian swung his axe. Together, we dug through the softer dirt under my paws to open a hole through to the lower levels.

I stuck my nose through and peered around. I could **HARDLY BELIEVE MY EYES!**

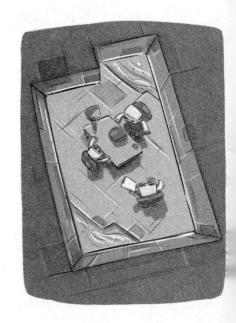

Between the underground rivers of lava, the baby turtles had set up **a complete laboratory.**

Some, wearing safety goggles and gloves, were carefully pouring lava from beakers onto turtle shell helmets—

# HISSSSSS!

Others were working on helmets at the smithing table, adding different combinations of diamond and netherite—

# BANG! BANG! BANG!

And others were taking notes on

clipboards, which would have been silent work, except that one turtle kept sneezing—

# WHAAA-CHOOO!

It was actually **adorable**. But the sound echoed around the underground chamber and became **loud and spooky.**

"Here are your **ghosts**," I whispered to Captain Hugo. "If they're still testing, it means they haven't worked out the **secret ingredient** to make turtle shell lava-resistant. Now, let's come up with a plan—"

Angrily, the captain **BANGED** his
sword against the ground.

"These are the ghosts who changed
all our passageways and stole our
things?" he yelled, and before I
could stop him, he and all the other
wither skeleton warriors **jumped**
down the hole.

## "WE HATE BEING INCONVENIENCED!"

They landed in the laboratory
and began running at the baby
turtle scientists, **shouting wildly.**
The baby turtles **shrieked** and

ran around in circles, knocking experiments into the lava rivers. All **evidence** of the turtles' plan was being destroyed by Captain Hugo's overexcited warriors.

Brian and I watched the chaos from the hole in the ceiling.

"Wow, wither skeletons aren't very **patient,** huh?" Brian commented.

We dropped down into the middle of the action. Wither skeletons were **swinging** their swords at fleeing baby turtles, and the turtles were madly digging with their tiny front paws, **burrowing** swiftly into the red earth. It was going to be over quickly, and once again the baby turtles were **going to get away.**

"Agent wolf cub."

I turned and spotted one final baby turtle, standing over an escape tunnel. No, not just any baby turtle—**the leader.**

## MY NEMESIS.

"You escaped my trap," it growled adorably. "Prepare to be **hypnotized.**"

It blinked slowly, eyes framed by long, sweet lashes, and the **cutest little smile** grew on its tiny face . . .

**"No way!"** I shouted, and both Brian and I activated our Anti-ADORBS collars. Little hearts burst into the air around us.

**We looked so cool!**

"This thing really does work!" Brian exclaimed.

My nemesis frowned dangerously. "You won't *always* have your friends to **watch your back**," it said. "You WON'T FOIL ME AGAIN."

I **pounced,** growling, but it slipped down the tiny hole and was gone.

"My friends and I will *always* watch each other's backs!" I shouted after it as the battle quietened down behind me. **"That's what friends do!"**

# THURSDAY

## LUNCHTIME

"Do you think we'll find the baby turtle leader again?" Brian asked.

We were walking back to our portal. Behind us was one turtle-free-and-ghost-free nether fortress, filled with **reluctantly grateful** wither skeletons. But we hadn't wanted to overstay our welcome.

"It's my nemesis, Brian," I explained

patiently. "Of course we will **cross paths again.** All secret agents have a nemesis. When you **grow up** into a secret agent, you'll get one too."

"Here we are—our hidden portal blocks." Brian started building us a new nether portal. "Four obsidian blocks along the bottom . . ."

"I don't think the baby turtles will show their faces around here again for a while though," I commented while he worked. "Captain Hugo and the wither skeletons were **quite terrifying.** And they said that all wither skeletons will continue to attack baby turtles in the future."

"Good thing we stopped them when we did," Brian agreed. "If they'd become lava-resistant, they'd be even **harder to defeat**. Okay. That's the last block. Now for **the flame!**"

Like before, the inside of the stone frame **burst** into swirling purple. I smiled at the vortex, glad to be going home. I'd **had enough** of the Nether, with its creepy darkness and hot, dusty air. And my stomach was rumbling. I was ready to go back to the Den and make dinner with my mom.

"Let's go before your nemesis comes back and destroys it again," Brian suggested. "It was such an **elaborate plan.** They *really* wanted to capture you."

I sighed. "I can't help being **so popular.**"

We stepped through the vortex to return to the Overworld.

I blinked, and when my eyes adjusted, I was surprised to see we'd arrived . . . on the **outskirts of an unfamiliar village.**

"Uh, Brian? This isn't where we **STARTED FROM."**

"**Oh, yeah.**" Brian scratched his neck sheepishly. "I forgot to mention, the dimensions don't **perfectly match up.** The distances are proportional at a one-to-eight ratio—"

"**I don't do math,**" I interrupted. "Are you telling me the nether portal just **dumped us** miles from my home?"

"Um . . . **yes.**"

"And now I have to *walk* all the way back?"

". . . **Yeah. Sorry.**"

I grinned with all my sharp, white teeth.

"Don't be," I said. "Just *think* of all the **POTENTIAL MISSIONS** we'll pass on the way!"

# JOIN WINSTON AND BRIAN IN THEIR NEXT TOP SECRET MINECRAFT MISSION:

# VILLAGE RESCUE

## BOOK 4 COMING SOON!

『TOP SECRET』

Ready for another mission, Winston?

You know I'm always ready for another chance to catch those villainous baby turtles in the act!

What if it's not baby turtles this time?

Pfft, Brian, please. It's almost like you haven't been reading my books.

You **HAVE** been reading my books, right?

Ehhh...